HOW DO YOU SHOP WITHOUT MONEY?

"Beth," Shawnie cried. "I figured out how you can get the new clothes!"

"You're kidding," Beth said, her heart skipping a beat. "How?"

Shawnie held out a small plastic card that had "Tanninger's" printed across it in bold letters. "My credit card! We'll put your clothes on my card at Tanninger's Department Store."

"I can't let your parents pay for my clothes," Beth replied doubtfully.

"They won't," Shawnie insisted. "The credit card bill comes later. That's when you pay me back. Don't you see? You pay me *later* instead of paying the store *now*."

Beth thought for a moment. It sounded great. She really *would* be paying for the clothes. She could have the clothes now, but pay for them when the bill came.

"Okay," Beth said, feeling an excited shiver rush up her spine. "And I promise, I'll pay you back right away!"

THE FABULOUS FIVE

Mall Mania

BETSY HAYNES

A BANTAM SKYLARK BOOK®
NEW YORK · TORONTO · LONDON · SYDNEY · AUCKLAND

RL 5, 009–012

MALL MANIA

A Bantam Skylark Book / March 1991

*Bantam Books are published by Bantam Books, a division of Ban-
tam Doubleday Dell Publishing Group, Inc. Its trademark,
consisting of the words "Bantam Books" and the portrayal of a
rooster, is Registered in U.S. Patent and Trademark Office and in
other countries. Marca Registrada. Bantam Books, 666 Fifth Ave-
nue, New York, New York 10103.*

PRINTED IN THE UNITED STATES OF AMERICA

CWO   0 9 8 7 6 5 4 3 2 1

Mall Mania

CHAPTER

1

"Wow, Beth!" cried Melanie. "We always knew you'd be a TV star. We just didn't know how soon!"

Beth Barry grinned at her four best friends, Melanie Edwards, Jana Morgan, Christie Winchell, and Katie Shannon. "When I signed up for Media Club, I thought we were just going to learn about television production," she said, her cheeks flushed with excitement. "But now there's a rumor that we might actually get to do something on cable."

Melanie gasped. "That's so exciting. Millions of people will be watching you."

Beth laughed and plucked nervously at a strand of

her short, spiky, brown hair. "It won't exactly be millions of people watching. We might get to do something on our local cable station."

Christie's eyes got big. "You'd really get to be on TV?"

Beth nodded. "Wouldn't that be terrific?"

"Awesome," Melanie whispered.

Beth glanced up at the clock in the hall. "It's almost time for the meeting. I'd better go."

"Good luck!" Katie said.

"We'll be thinking about you," chimed in Christie.

"Should I get your autograph now or later?" Jana asked. "I want to be sure to get the first one."

"How about later?" Beth said, grinning. "See you guys tomorrow."

Melanie gave her a thumbs-up sign for luck. Beth waved good-bye and then pushed open the door to the media center.

Mrs. Karl, the media specialist, was standing at the tall desk just inside the door, checking books out to a line of students.

"Excuse me, Mrs. Karl," Beth said. "Could you tell me where the Media Club is meeting?"

Mrs. Karl smiled and pointed to a sign on the front of the desk. The large letters had been printed in purple ink.

LIGHTS! CAMERAS! ACTION!
Want to be a TV star? Want to learn what goes on behind
the scenes in a TV studio?
Join the Media Club!
First meeting: Monday, after school.
          Production room of media center.

Beth thanked Mrs. Karl, then headed toward the production room in the back. She opened the door and walked in.

The production room was usually used for things such as recording educational TV programs, laminating posters, and storing film projectors and video cameras used in the classrooms. But for the purpose of the new Media Club, all the equipment had been moved to the side. A circle of chairs had been set up in the middle of the room, and most of them already were occupied by students.

Mr. Levine looked up from one of the chairs and smiled.

"Come on in, Beth," he said. "We're about to begin."

Beth slid into a seat next to Shawnie Pendergast and smiled hello. As Shawnie smiled back, Beth couldn't help thinking with a tinge of envy that Shawnie looked as gorgeous as always. She was wearing a yellow-and-white minidress, and her long, blond hair was tied back in a yellow ribbon. Beth had always admired her clothes. Shawnie never seemed to wear anything twice.

"This is going to be *great*!" Shawnie whispered.

"I know," Beth said. "I can't wait to hear about everything we're going to do!"

Paul Smoke, a ninth-grader, whom she'd gotten to know during rehearsals for Wakeman Junior High's Halloween play, was sitting next to Shawnie, and next to him was Shane Arrington. Melanie might be tempted to sign up for the Media Club when she finds out Shane's a member, mused Beth. Melanie had just started to date Shane, and she was totally crazy about him. The other people present were Funny Hawthorne, a good friend of Jana's; Jon Smith, who was in a few of her classes; and Tim Riggs, an eighth-grader.

"Just to make sure you're in the right place," began Mr. Levine, "this is Wakeman's new Media Club. We're going to learn a lot about putting together videotapes for TV."

"Are the rumors true?" Funny asked. "Will we get to be on TV?"

Mr. Levine smiled. "Good news travels fast. I just got the go-ahead for the show yesterday."

"A *show*?" said Shawnie, her eyes wide. "A real TV show?"

"That's right," Mr. Levine replied. "We're going to produce a regular fifteen-minute spot on Spectrum, our local cable company."

"Wow!" Paul said. There were murmurs of excitement from everyone.

"It'll air every Saturday morning at ten o'clock," continued Mr. Levine.

"You mean, I'll have to get up *early* to see it?" Funny said, grinning.

"Ten o'clock is early?" asked Mr. Levine.

"Not for me!" cried Shawnie. "Ten is when I hit the mall!"

Beth smiled at Shawnie's outburst. Beth loved to shop, too, and even had a sign on the bulletin board in her room that said, WHEN THE GOING GETS TOUGH, THE TOUGH GO SHOPPING. But she would definitely stay home from the mall to see a show the club had produced!

"This should be a fun project," said Mr. Levine. "We'll be reporting on school news, sports scores, upcoming events, school menus—"

"So everyone will know when to bring lunch from home!" Funny interrupted. Her infectious giggle made

everybody laugh along with her. She made a face.
"Have you ever had the school's goulash? Gross."

"We're also going to have a special ecology segment,"
Mr. Levine went on. "We'll give viewers suggestions
about what they can do to recycle and help save our
environment."

"Great idea," Beth said. "We're really going to be
giving out some helpful information." She paused for a
second. "What will the name of the show be?"

Mr. Levine looked around the circle. "What do you
think of *The Wakeman Bulletin Board*?"

"That's great!" Funny said. "That's exactly what
we'll be doing: posting information!"

"I like that name, too," Beth said. The other kids
nodded.

"Where do we start?" asked Shane.

"I'm going to assign your jobs next." Mr. Levine
glanced down at a clipboard in his lap. "We'll rotate on-
camera and off-camera jobs every month so everyone
will learn as much as possible. Beth and Shawnie, why
don't you take the co-anchor jobs first?"

Beth's stomach did a flip-flop. It would be like co-
anchoring the news! She thought, Wait till I tell the
rest of The Fabulous Five that I'm going to have a
chance to be on camera!

"There is one other on-camera job," said Mr.

Levine. "That will be the ecology reporter." He looked around the circle and stopped at Paul Smoke. "Paul, why don't you take that assignment first?"

"Great," Paul said. "I've got some ideas already."

Beth smiled. Paul had done a terrific act with his pet bats for the Halloween show, and she'd bet that he did have good ideas for the TV show, too.

"Terrific," said Mr. Levine. "Who would like to be the cameraperson for this first month?"

"I would," Jon volunteered.

"Good," Mr. Levine said, and made a note on his paper. "Now we'll need a director. That will be a very important job. The director will organize the whole show, decide what will go first and second, and so on. The director will oversee the program from start to finish."

"I'll do that," Funny said.

"Fine," said Mr. Levine. "Shane and Tim, we won't have a show if there's nothing to report. So I'd like you two to collect information. Menus, sports scores, upcoming dances, that sort of thing."

The boys nodded.

"Sure," replied Tim.

"Our first show will air this week, so we have some very busy days ahead of us," said Mr. Levine. "We'll shoot the spot on Friday after school. Are there any problems with your schedules?"

All the club members shook their heads, and Mr. Levine nodded. "Good."

"Where will we shoot the show?" Jon asked.

"That's a good question." Mr. Levine thought for a moment. "Since we don't have a set ready, and since this room really isn't very appropriate—" He looked around the room. "In fact, this would be a terrible place. It's quiet, but pretty ugly. Do you have any suggestions?"

"How about the main media center?" asked Jon. "It's carpeted, and there are nice-looking, comfortable chairs in the magazine area. We could make it look like those morning news sets where they have coffee cups sitting on little tables in front of the anchors."

Mr. Levine beamed. "Great idea, Jon."

"And I know some of the lighting guys down at the TV station," Jon offered. "I'll bet they'd come here on our first shoot day and advise us about setting up our lights."

"Wow, that's great!" said Paul.

Beth nodded her approval. Jon would be a big help to the club. His parents were Chip Smith, a sports director for the local TV station, and Marge Whitworth, the news anchorperson. He knew all kinds of things about TV production.

A tingle ran up Beth's spine as she glanced around the room again. Actually, everyone at the meeting had lots to contribute to the project. She had a feeling that *The Wakeman Bulletin Board* was going to be a big hit!

CHAPTER

"*W*hat are you going to wear on the show?" Shawnie asked Beth. "We should coordinate our outfits."

The two girls were walking down the hall after the meeting.

The question stopped Beth cold. She had been so carried away with the idea of the club's putting on a real TV show and her own assignment as co-anchor that the idea of what she would wear on-camera hadn't even occurred to her. She shivered as she thought about it now. She loved her own kooky wardrobe, of course, but the wild prints and neon colors would never do if she was to look sophisticated and professional. To make matters worse, Shawnie had one of the most fabulous wardrobes in school. Next to Shawnie's, Beth's own clothes would look positively awful.

"I don't know," Beth murmured. "I guess I need something new."

"Great!" said Shawnie. "Let's go shopping together!"

Beth brightened. "That's a good idea." She winced as she realized that her allowance was gone and that she had spent her emergency savings on two tapes the week before. Oh, well, she thought. I'll talk to Mom. Maybe she'll help me out.

"Terrific!" said Shawnie. "I'll get my mom to pick you up after supper, about seven. We'll go to the mall. Mom'll probably hang around," she added, rolling her eyes, "but we'll just park her somewhere with a soda and head off to shop our brains out! We'll look through every single store and then pick our favorite outfits. We'll be dynamite."

"Yeah," Beth said uncertainly.

"See you at seven," Shawnie called as she dashed off to her locker.

Beth nodded and headed for home.

"She can't have a new outfit!" Brittany wailed. "I have to pay for all of *my* clothes that aren't absolutely essential!

And I started earning my clothes money when I was *her* age!"

Brittany, Beth's sixteen-year-old sister, had walked into the kitchen during Beth's plea to her mother. Now she was standing in the middle of the room, her eyes blazing.

Beth whirled around and faced Brittany angrily. "Mind your own business!" she snapped. "This has nothing to do with you!"

Mrs. Barry stopped slicing the apple she was going to add to the dinner's fruit salad. "Girls, stop arguing!" she said.

"Sorry, Mom." Beth lowered her voice. "But I was wondering if I could get a little advance on my allowance—"

"Absolutely not!" Brittany cried. "I never got an advance on *my* allow—"

"Brittany," Mrs. Barry interrupted. "Please remove yourself from this kitchen right now."

Brittany let out an exasperated breath and stomped out of the room.

"Mom—" Beth began.

"Honey," her mother said, "the reason we give you an allowance is so you will learn how to budget for yourself."

"But I've learned how to do that," Beth insisted.

"And this is very important. I'm going to be on *cable*!"

"And that's very exciting," her mother said gently. "But I'm not going to give you an advance on your allowance, honey. Between paying off Todd's braces and having the house painted last month, we just don't have any extra to spend right now."

Beth felt her face fall practically to the floor.

"What about your blue dress? It looks wonderful on you," her mother suggested.

"I can't wear that!" Beth wailed. "I need something that's—well, *cool*! You know, Mom! I need something really professional and wonderful!"

"What about doing some baby-sitting?" asked Mrs. Barry. "You could earn some money to buy a new outfit that way."

"But we're shooting the first spot on Friday!" Beth moaned. "There isn't *time* to get a baby-sitting job and buy the perfect outfit by then! I need to start shopping tonight!"

"I'm sorry," Mrs. Barry said, "but the answer is no." She turned back to her fruit salad.

Beth knew that it was pointless to argue any further. When her mother said, "The answer is no," that meant the discussion was over.

Beth hung her head and left the kitchen with a heavy heart.

"I knew she wouldn't let you get a new outfit," Brittany called triumphantly from the dining room.

"You were eavesdropping!" Beth said.

"Yup."

Beth stormed upstairs and threw herself across her bed. Why did her younger brother have to have braces, anyway? she thought. And even though there had been little curlicues of paint flaking off the house, it hadn't needed painting *that* badly! Getting a new outfit was *far* more important than those dumb things!

Suddenly she sat upright. What was she going to tell Shawnie? She and her mother would be coming by at seven o'clock to pick Beth up for shopping. Beth had to call her and tell her she couldn't go.

Beth got up and walked to her parents' bedroom, then sat on the bed, staring at the phone. What should she say? That she didn't have the money and that her parents couldn't afford new clothes because of *braces* and *house paint*? It would be embarrassing to admit that to someone like Shawnie, whose parents had lots of money, even though it was the truth.

Beth sighed deeply. She really *didn't* have the money, and her parents wouldn't lend it to her. There didn't seem to be any alternative. She would have to tell Shawnie the truth.

Beth looked up Shawnie's number in the phone book. Shawnie had her own line, of course. Shawnie had *everything*!

She dialed the number and listened to the ring. Maybe, Beth thought hopefully, Shawnie wouldn't answer and Beth could just leave the message that she couldn't go shopping tonight.

Don't be there, don't be there, Beth repeated to herself.

Click.

"Hello?"

"Shawnie?" said Beth, her heart sinking. "Hi. This is Beth." She took a deep breath, then told Shawnie she couldn't go shopping and explained why.

"Oh, that's too bad," Shawnie said, sounding disappointed. "We really need to be coordinated."

"I know," said Beth.

"So, what are you going to wear?" Shawnie asked. "I'll work around you."

"I don't know," Beth said. "I have no idea."

"Well," Shawnie said, "maybe we could go through your closet and find something that isn't—well, isn't too wild."

Beth flinched. Shawnie obviously didn't think much of Beth's wardrobe. Actually, Beth's clothes were pretty funky, just not right for TV. And not expensive, like Shawnie's.

"I don't know," Beth said.

"Well, you have to wear *something*!" Shawnie insisted.

"I know," said Beth. She felt miserable and just wanted to end the conversation. "Uh, Shawnie, I have to go now and help Mom with supper."

"Oh," said Shawnie. "Okay."

Beth said good-bye and hung up, blinking back tears. She stretched out on her parents' bed and buried her face in her arms.

This show was the biggest thing that had ever happened to her. It was her big chance to get experience in front of a television camera and show the world that she had talent. But instead of being ecstatic, she felt awful. Deborah Norville didn't wear stirrup pants and hand-painted sweatshirts on *Today*. Neither did Joan Lunden on *Good Morning America*. What was she going to do?

There just *had* to be a way she could get some new clothes!

CHAPTER

3

*B*eth carried her cereal bowl into the family room the next morning and flipped on the TV, tuning in *Good Morning America*. She sat down on the ottoman directly across from the set and waited impatiently while co-anchor Charles Gibson interviewed the author of a best-selling spy novel.

It might have been better for me to have a boy for my co-anchor, she thought miserably. At least with Shane or Tim I wouldn't have to worry about coordinating my wardrobe.

Just then the camera shifted to Joan Lunden, and Beth stopped her spoon in midair, letting her breath out slowly as she stared at the screen. "Wow," she whispered softly, "is she ever classy."

For the next few minutes Beth sat transfixed, watching Ms. Lunden's every move as she talked to her co-host and interviewed guests on the program. Beth raked her fingers through her own short, spiky hair and looked longingly at Joan's long, silky blond hair. Next Beth's attention shifted to the softly tailored turquoise jacket and paisley blouse the co-anchor wore, and to her delicately manicured fingernails.

"Oh, I'll never be like that," Beth moaned. "Never, never."

Sure you can, said a little voice in her brain. *All you need is some practice.*

Beth put her cereal bowl on the floor and arranged herself in the same position as Joan Lunden. Then she tilted her head just as Joan Lunden was tilting hers and reached out a hand, perfectly imitating the gesture the coanchor was making on the screen. Miming was easy, she soon discovered. If she concentrated hard, she could even lip-synch and lag only a fraction of a second behind.

This is what it's going to feel like to be in front of the camera, Beth thought with excitement. Smiling, she nodded graciously to her cohost. Then a loud voice boomed behind her.

"Hey, Beth. Have you flipped, or what?"

Beth whirled around, her face flaming in embarrassment. Her younger brother stood leaning against the door frame with a smirk on his face.

"Oh, I get it," he said. "Now that you've landed a big part on TV, you're sizing up the competition." He threw back his head and laughed. "Lots of luck," he called as he strolled away.

Beth let out a sigh of exasperation and glanced once more at Joan Lunden before turning off the set. Todd could laugh all he wanted to, she thought angrily, but she was going to be a star!

Shawnie was waiting just inside the school gate when Beth arrived that morning.

"Beth," she said, "I had the greatest idea after I went to bed last night. I was so excited, it took me an hour to get to sleep! I figured out how you can get the new clothes!"

"You're kidding," said Beth, her heart skipping a beat as the image of Joan Lunden in her turquoise jacket and paisley blouse filled her mind. "How?"

"Voilà!" Shawnie said. "My credit card!"

Beth frowned, not understanding.

"Don't you get it?" asked Shawnie. "We'll put your clothes on my credit card at Tanninger's."

"*Your* card?" Beth asked, still not quite believing. "You have your own credit card?"

Shawnie held it out. "Just look at the name," she said proudly.

Beth leaned in closer. Sure enough, the name stamped on the department store's card was SHAWNIE PENDERGAST.

"Wow," Beth said. "And you pay for all your own clothes?"

Shawnie laughed. "Of course not," she said. "My *parents* do. It's part of the payoff for their not being around me very much."

Beth understood. Shawnie's parents both had high-paying jobs, and they worked all day and spent a great deal of time away from her. They were also very strict about where she could go and what she could do. Since they weren't around to supervise her comings and goings, they didn't let her leave the house very often. So they paid her off by spoiling her and showering her with material things, even her own credit card. Beth knew that some department stores would issue cards to kids if their parents consented and took responsibility for paying the bills, but she had never actually seen a kid's card before.

"I can't let your parents pay for my clothes," said Beth.

"They won't," Shawnie insisted. "The credit card bill comes later. That's when you pay me back. Don't you see? You pay *me* later instead of paying the store *now*."

Beth thought a moment. It sounded great. She really *would* be paying for the clothes. She could have the clothes now, but pay for them when the bill came.

"Okay," Beth said, feeling a shiver of excitement. "And I promise, I'll pay you back right away!"

"Hey, don't sweat it," Shawnie said. "Let's head for the mall right after Media Club this afternoon. Maybe we can find our outfits today."

"Great!" said Beth. "I can't wait!"

Beth said good-bye to Shawnie and hurried to the fence to find the rest of The Fabulous Five. She had called each of her friends the night before to tell them her big news about the cable show and ask them for suggestions about what she should wear on-camera. Nobody had any ideas. Christie's clothes were the perfect style, but she was too tall. Katie was a size smaller than Beth. Melanie's wardrobe was too frilly, and Jana's was too conservative.

But now Beth had found the perfect solution to her problem. Or, at least, Shawnie had found it for her, and she raced to tell her friends that she was going to get her new clothes after all!

*　*　*

"That's *incredible*!" said Shawnie, looking at Beth's reflection in the three-way mirror in the dressing room. "It's the *perfect* outfit for the show!"

Beth looked at herself appraisingly in the mirror. The dress really did look great on her. It had a short, straight, black skirt that fit well on her narrow hips and a wide, red belt that flattered her small waistline. The collar was red and black, and stood up high around her neck.

Shawnie grinned. "It's classy and flattering and professional and—"

"And expensive!" Beth burst out, looking for the first time at the price tag.

"Oh, it's not *that* expensive. Don't worry about it!" Shawnie said, waving her hand. "The important thing is that we found the perfect outfit for you!"

Beth did some quick math in her head. Shawnie was right, she decided. It would take some work, but she could get the dress paid for in maybe four weekends of baby-sitting.

"And now you need some shoes," said Shawnie.

"Oh, no," said Beth. "I think I'd better stop here."

"Then at least some earrings," Shawnie said. "Those will show up when the camera zooms in on your face."

"Well, maybe you're right about that," Beth conceded. "I'll see if I can find some inexpensive ones."

The girls bought the dress with Shawnie's credit card and headed for the jewelry department. They wandered along the glass counter and examined the earring displays.

"Oh, wow," Shawnie said. "These gold ones are beautiful!" She pulled them off the display rack.

"Yes, they are," agreed Beth. "They'd go perfectly with my dress. How much?"

Shawnie turned them over in her hand and showed the price to Beth.

"No," said Beth. "That's way too much. Let's keep looking."

Shawnie shrugged and put the gold ones back. The girls continued their walk along the counter.

"Look!" cried Beth. "Here is a red pair that'll go great with my dress!"

"Perrrfect!" Shawnie cooed. "And not expensive."

"Great," said Beth. She grabbed Shawnie's charge card and handed it to the salesclerk. "I'll take these."

"Now we have to find something for me," Shawnie said excitedly. "It *has* to go with your outfit."

"Right." Beth grinned. "What a great team we'll be!"

"I should have a red dress," Shawnie said. She

looked at her watch. "But I'd better not get it today. Mom thinks I'm at home starting on homework. She'll be there in a half hour, and I'd better be there!"

"Okay," Beth said.

Obviously, Shawnie was still sneaking around. Beth felt sorry that Shawnie had to do that. Once Shawnie had run away and stayed in Katie's basement because she was angry that her parents wouldn't let her go on a march for hunger with a lot of Wakeman kids. Beth had thought Shawnie and her parents had resolved all that, but apparently there were still a few problems. She also could imagine how frustrated Shawnie was, having parents who seldom let her do things, but sometimes Shawnie's reactions really went off the deep end.

"Are you sure your parents won't mind that I used your charge card?" Beth asked her.

"No, they never care about stuff like that," Shawnie assured her. "Just so I'm home on time!" She laughed.

"Well, it was really nice of you to let me use it," Beth said.

"No problem," said Shawnie. "See you tomorrow."

Beth walked home and through the front door. She heard noises in the kitchen and decided her mother was working on dinner preparation. She scooted up the stairs, not wanting to answer questions about the Tanninger's bag.

Her mother surprised her when she walked out of her bedroom just as Beth reached the top of the stairs.

"Hi, honey," her mother said. "I expected you nearly an hour ago. Did your Media Club meeting run long today?"

"Um, yes, it did," Beth said, crossing her fingers behind her back. *It had run a couple of minutes longer than usual*, she thought.

"What's in the bag?" her mother asked.

Slowly, Beth opened the bag and held it up for her mother to peek inside. She hoped none of the tags showed.

"Uh, I was with Shawnie Pendergast this afternoon," Beth said. "Doesn't she have great taste?"

"Oh, is she letting you wear that dress for the TV show?" Mrs. Barry asked.

Beth nodded, hoping her mother wouldn't notice the red flush creeping across her face.

"How nice of her!" said Mrs. Barry. "See, it all worked out after all, didn't it?"

"Yeah, it did," murmured Beth.

Her mother started down the stairs. "I've got Brittany working on supper," she called back over her shoulder. "Should be ready in half an hour."

"Great," said Beth.

She walked into her room and sat on the bed. She took out the dress and held it up. It was as beautiful as she had thought it was in the store.

"And it looks even better *on*," she whispered.

Beth stood in front of the mirror and held the dress up to her. It really was perfect!

Then she thought of the conversation with her mother. She hadn't exactly told any lies.

She gazed into her own eyes, and a wave of guilt washed over her. She may not have told an out-and-out lie, but she had led her mother to believe something that wasn't true. Wasn't that the same thing as a lie?

She closed her eyes a moment, and when she opened them, she looked away from the mirror. She shouldn't have done it, but it had been necessary, she told herself.

She *needed* this dress!

CHAPTER

4

"Last night I was watching Connie Chung on television, and I decided that I like her style better than Joan Lunden's," Beth said to Jana and Katie as they made their way through the crowded halls after school.

"I thought Joan Lunden was your idol," Jana said.

Beth shrugged. "You ought to watch Connie Chung sometime. I mean, she is so professional and businesslike. Joan Lunden is awfully casual. Watching her is almost like having your aunt come for a visit or something."

"Personally, I like Barbara Walters," Katie chimed in. "Now there's someone who's professional and businesslike."

Beth made a face and started to reply to Katie when she caught sight of Shawnie in the crowd ahead. "I've got to run," she said instead. "I have to talk to Shawnie before the Media Club meeting starts."

"See you later," said Jana.

"Shawnie?" Beth called, hurrying up behind her.

Shawnie turned and, seeing Beth, broke into a grin. "Hi."

"Hi," said Beth. "You know, I was thinking last night and decided that maybe you were right about those shoes. I really don't have a pair that would be quite right."

"Okay," replied Shawnie. "Come with me to the mall again after the meeting, and we'll pick up a pair of shoes before we get a new outfit for me."

Beth grinned. "I really appreciate what you're doing for me, Shawnie. And I promise you'll get paid back right away."

"Hey," Shawnie said, smiling. "Do I look worried?"

Beth giggled. "Nope. Not at all."

"Come on," Shawnie said. "Let's get to the meeting."

The girls hurried into the media room and slipped into their seats just as Mr. Levine was starting the meeting.

"Okay," said the teacher, "we'd better get going. I'll turn this meeting over to our director. Funny?"

Funny Hawthorne cleared her throat. "Okay, everybody, this is Wednesday, and we shoot on Friday, so let's see how everyone is doing. I need progress reports from each one of you. First, Shane and Tim, have you collected the information that our co-anchors can report on?"

"We've got last week's basketball scores," answered Tim, "next week's menu, and a couple of upcoming school events—like the band concert, the next basketball game, and the school dance—to tell about."

"Good," said Funny. "Get that information to me before you leave, will you? I'll need to write the script tonight."

"Sure," said Shane. "It's all here on this list." He took a sheet of paper out of his backpack and handed it to Funny. He grinned. "And if you ever want a fascinating interview subject, I can always get Igor in here. He's very articulate and impressive—"

"Uh-huh," Funny said, smiling at the mention of Shane's pet iguana.

"The publicity might entice some female iguana to call—" Shane continued.

"Yeah, right, okay," Funny said, laughing and waving at him to be quiet. "You guys did a good job. What about you, Jon?"

"I talked to Wayne Paulsen at my parents' station," Jon responded. "He told me he'd be glad to show up here after school on Friday and advise us on the lights."

"Excellent!" Funny announced, then turned to Paul Smoke. "What are you going to do in your ecology segment?"

Paul smiled. "I'm going to talk about bats."

"*Bats?*" said Funny. "What do bats have to do with ecology?"

Paul's eyebrows shot up. "Everything! More people should know that."

"Are you going to bring one of your bats?" Funny asked.

"Of course," Paul said. He grinned and seemed to loosen up a little. "Robin. He's the ham of the family."

Funny laughed. "Was he the one that made the surprise entrance during the Halloween show?"

"The very one," Paul replied. "He loves the spotlight."

"Whatever you say," said Funny. "We'll save five minutes for your segment."

"Let me interrupt here to say something about timing," said Mr. Levine. "Timing is crucial in both TV and radio. Spectrum Cable is giving us exactly fifteen minutes. We should wrap up and end the program about a half second before that time is up. They will cut us off at exactly fifteen minutes, so it's better to be a half second short than a half second over."

Beth was fascinated. She had no idea timing was so critical.

"We'll need to put together some music at the top and bottom," Mr. Levine continued. "And we'll have a sign to open the show, since we don't have the technology to flash Chyrons over the screen."

"What are Chyrons?" asked Beth.

Jon sat up. "You know when someone is being interviewed on TV, and at the bottom of the screen you see the name of that person?"

"Right," Beth said.

"Those letters are called Chyrons," he finished. "You see them a lot in commercials, too, when, say, the date of a sale is thrown up on the screen. Or the name of the store having the sale."

"Oh, yeah, now I know what you mean," Beth said, nodding. It made her feel so professional. Of course Connie Chung and Joan Lunden knew about Chyrons.

"Anyway," said Mr. Levine, "since we've had just a few days to prepare for this first show, Jon and I already got together and chose some theme music. I brought a tape of it, and I'll give you a chance to hear it."

He flipped a switch on the tape recorder in front of him, and the music began. It was light and upbeat. The club members looked at one another and grinned.

"That's perfect!" said Beth.

"Yeah, I like it." Shane snapped his fingers to the beat.

And suddenly it was over.

"That's the shortest music I've ever heard!" remarked Shawnie.

Mr. Levine chuckled. "It's supposed to be short. It's production music. Stations buy tapes filled with short bits of production music for commercials and for introducing this type of program. Production music comes in ten-, fifteen-, thirty-, and sixty-second segments."

"And you can get longer music for films," Jon added.

"Awesome!" said Funny.

"Right," said Jon. "That way, you don't have to have someone compose and perform music for you for local TV or radio. That would be too expensive, anyway."

"This show is going to be so great!" exclaimed Beth.

"Yes, it is," agreed Funny. "I'll get you co-anchors your scripts by tomorrow so that you can become familiar with them. I don't think you'll need to memorize them, but you should have them very well in mind."

"Sure," Beth said, but she had every intention of memorizing her script!

"Shane and Tim," Mr. Levine said, "I'm going to put you two in charge of making posters to put up around school advertising our show on Saturday."

"Good idea," said Funny. "We want everybody in the school to be watching."

Beth's stomach did a flip-flop. *The whole school will be watching!* She thought of the kids in her classes and her teachers all sitting in front of their TV sets. And then she thought of her boyfriend, Keith Masterson, and her heartbeat quickened.

Keith would be watching for sure!

Beth took a deep breath. She was going to practice and practice and practice! She'd be the *best* co-anchor on cable TV!

"Oh, those shoes are so *cool!*" said Beth, looking at the reflection of her feet in the small mirror that stood on the floor at Tanninger's. She had never seen Joan Lunden's or Connie Chung's shoes since she had begun watching their programs, but she was sure their shoes matched their outfits just as perfectly as these matched hers.

"They're just what you need," Shawnie agreed. "I love them!"

The low-heeled shoes were red with a thin line of

black trim. Beth took off the left one and held it up, looking at it critically. "I can't think of one other thing I could wear these with, though," she said.

"So what?" Shawnie asked. "You couldn't have found a better pair of shoes for the show."

Beth hesitated for another moment. She really should put them back, she thought. But they *were* right for the show. She had to have them.

"Okay," she said. "I'll take them."

Shawnie handed her the credit card.

Beth squared her shoulders and marched to the sales counter, handing the card to the clerk.

"Oh, I just love my new outfit!" Beth hugged herself with joy.

"Isn't this fun?" said Shawnie. "Whenever I'm feeling down, I just go shopping!" She thought for a moment, then added, "In fact, whenever I'm feeling up, I go shopping, too. Shopping just gives me a *high*, you know what I mean?"

"I do now!" said Beth.

After Shawnie signed for Beth's shoes, the girls hurried to the juniors department to find a new outfit for Shawnie.

"Red," Shawnie declared. "It's got to be red."

"Okay!" Beth shouted. "One red outfit, coming up!"

Dancing through the racks of clothes, she pulled out

a red satin prom dress trimmed in shimmering sequins. Laughing, she held it up to Shawnie. "How about this one?"

Shawnie blinked in surprise and then laughed back. "No, no. That's too casual. Put it back." Then Shawnie raced ahead of Beth to the sportswear department and held up a tomato-red ski parka with matching bibs. "What do you think of this?"

Both girls were laughing like crazy, pulling one red outfit after another off the racks and holding them up in front of Shawnie.

"Uh-oh," said Beth, looking around the department. "I think the clerks are looking at us funny."

Shawnie nodded. "Right. I guess I'd better get serious about finding a dress."

In five minutes, Shawnie had collected five dresses to try on. And in another ten, she had chosen her favorite to wear with Beth on the show.

"All right, Beth!" Shawnie exclaimed. "Now we will be color-coordinated!"

Shawnie signed for her dress, and the girls headed out of the juniors department giggling. The only department between Juniors and the mall entrance was the china and fine gifts department.

"Oooh, Beth," cried Shawnie, "wouldn't this look terrific sitting on the table in front of us?"

Beth gasped. Sitting on a little display table on top of a lacy tablecloth was a beautiful ceramic teapot, surrounded by six fragile cups and saucers.

"These would give us the perfect touch of elegance!" Shawnie said, her eyes still glued to the display.

"They sure would," agreed Beth. "But we can't afford them, too."

Shawnie thought a minute. "There's just *got* to be a way we could buy these. Wait, I know! What if you bought the teapot and I bought the cups and saucers?"

"I don't know," Beth said doubtfully.

"After the show is over," said Shawnie, "we could put them away and give them to our moms for Christmas! Moms love this kind of stuff."

Beth considered that. "Well, I guess they *would* be good Christmas gifts," she admitted.

"They sure would," Shawnie said.

Beth began to smile. "Boy, this would look so great sitting in front of us on the table."

"You've got it." Shawnie looked at Beth. "What do you say?"

"I say," Beth said with a grin, "CHARGE IT!"

CHAPTER

"*W*hat's that?" asked Jana.

It was Friday morning before school. Students were milling around the locker area, talking and getting ready to go to their first classes. Jana and Beth stood in front of Beth's open locker.

"What's what?" asked Beth.

Jana pointed to the Tanninger's packages sitting at the bottom of Beth's locker. "What's in the packages?"

"It's my new outfit for the show," said Beth. "We're taping today after school. Want to see?"

"Are you kidding?" said Jana, grinning. "Of course!"

Beth smiled and rolled her eyes dramatically. "It's

incredible, wonderful, *gorgeous*! What more can I say?" She reached into the bag, pulled out the dress, and held it up next to her.

"Wow!" said Jana. "You're right. It *is* incredible!"

"And wonderful and gorgeous, right?" Beth prodded, grinning.

"And more," Jana replied.

Beth took her new shoes out of the box and held them up next to the dress. "Are they perfect, or what?"

"They're awesome!" exclaimed Jana. "Beth, you're going to look wonderful on TV!"

Beth sighed and smiled. "I sure hope so." She couldn't help noticing that several of the girls walking down the hall slowed down to stare at her and her new dress.

They're so envious! Beth thought. I really am lucky to have the chance to be on TV, and to have a great new dress to wear.

Jana saw the tag dangling from the dress and scooped it up in her hand. She turned it over and read the price.

"Wow!" She looked up at Beth, astonished. "Are your parents buying this for you?"

"Nope," said Beth. "I'm buying it for me. Shawnie bought it with her credit card, and I'm paying her back."

Jana looked astonished. "She has her own credit card?"

Beth nodded. "Isn't she lucky?"

Jana looked at Beth with concern. "How are you going to get the money to pay her back?"

Beth shrugged. "I'll just get some extra baby-sitting jobs and add what I make to my allowance. I'll get the dress paid for by the end of the month. Well, maybe a little after."

"Those are going to have to be some super-long baby-sitting jobs," said Jana, shaking her head.

"I know," Beth admitted. "But I just *had* to get a new outfit. Nothing I had was right."

"*Whoa!*" a chorus of voices sounded behind them.

Beth turned to find Melanie, Christie, and Katie standing wide-eyed, staring at her dress.

"Where did you get that *beautiful* dress!" Melanie cried.

Beth smiled and explained her deal with Shawnie.

"Of *course* Shawnie has her own charge card!" Melanie said, throwing up her hands. "I should have known that!"

"Oh, Beth," Christie said. "It's really terrific. You'll look gorgeous in it."

"Thanks, guys," Beth said.

"So what do your parents think about your using Shawnie's credit card?" Katie asked.

Beth lowered her eyes. "Well, to tell you the truth, my parents don't exactly know about my deal with Shawnie. They think I'm borrowing the dress from her."

Jana frowned. "Won't they be angry when they find out?"

Beth sighed. "If I can get the outfit paid for pretty soon, I'll just explain to them that I *earned* it."

"I hope you'll be able to pay for it as easily as you think you will," Jana said.

"It'll be okay," Beth reassured her. "So I'll have to work for a while to pay for it. It's worth it!"

Melanie glanced down at Beth's locker again. "What else is in there?" she asked.

"Wait till you see this!" Beth declared. She took the teapot out of its box and held it up for the girls to admire. "We're going to have this on the coffee table in front of us! Isn't it wonderful?"

"It's just the right touch," Christie said, nodding.

"Shawnie got some teacups that match," Beth added.

"Are you going to pay Shawnie for the teapot, too?" Katie asked her.

"Sure," answered Beth. "Then I'm going to save it and give it to my mom for Christmas."

"Great idea," said Melanie.

"Well, we can't wait to see the show," offered Jana.

"I know," Beth said excitedly. "Why don't you guys come over tomorrow and watch it with me? Come at nine o'clock, and I'll make pancakes before the show."

"Sounds great to me," said Katie, and the others said they would be there, too.

Beth watched the clock all day. She tried to concentrate on classwork, but all she could think of was the taping of *The Wakeman Bulletin Board* after school. Every time she looked at the clock on the classroom wall, expecting twenty minutes to have gone by, she discovered that only a couple of minutes had passed. The day dragged on endlessly.

At last the dismissal bell rang. Her heart racing, Beth ran to her locker and picked up her new outfit and the teapot. She rushed into the girls' room to get ready for the taping of the show.

The bathroom was empty. Beth took her makeup case out of her book bag with trembling hands. She didn't usually use a lot of makeup, but she knew that the bright lights would make her face look washed out if she didn't apply some color and highlights.

First Beth applied the foundation, smoothing it over her face and blending the edges into her hairline. Then she put some eyeshadow on her lids and darkened her lashes with mascara. After that came blush and lip gloss. Finally a dusting of powder took the shine from her nose and chin.

She pulled the dress out of the bag and slipped it on over her head. With a pounding heart, she zipped up the back and straightened the fabric so that it hung smoothly. Next, she put on the shoes and the earrings that matched the dress so perfectly.

Beth stood in front of the mirror and looked at her reflection. It was perfect. The absolutely right outfit for her television debut. Her heart was really racing now. *This is ridiculous*, Beth thought. *I've acted in lots of plays. This is a taped show. Why does it feel like such a big deal?*

Then she remembered the thousands of people who might tune in to see her on TV. *The show was a big deal!*

She took a deep breath, and gazed at herself in the mirror. "You look terrific. You know your lines. And you're going to be just as good as they are," she whispered to her reflection as she thought about the women she had been watching on TV and whose techniques she had been studying. "Not only that, *someday* you might be one of *them*." Beth smiled at herself and started to leave the rest room. Then she stopped, turned around, and gave herself a big grin. "Break a leg!" she shouted, and then raced out the door.

When Beth arrived at the media center, Shawnie looked up, obviously relieved. "Oh, good. You're all ready. I changed in the bathroom across the hall."

Shawnie looked terrific in her new red dress and matching shoes. She wore a gold chain with a crystal pendant around her neck. She grinned and stepped up next to Beth, putting an arm around Beth's shoulder. "Do we look *great* together, or what?"

"Sensational!" Beth said. "Now if I can just stop shaking . . ."

"Why be nervous?" Shawnie asked, sounding full of confidence. "We look so good that if we do mess up, no one will even notice—they'll be too busy gawking at these gorgeous women on the screen in front of them!"

Beth nodded. They did look great together, and she'd spent all last night going over the script, but she still didn't feel as calm as Shawnie sounded.

The media center had closed five minutes earlier to anyone not involved in the cable program. Mr. Levine, Jon, and a tall, lanky man with dark hair were setting up the lights.

"That must be the guy from the TV station," Beth whispered to Shawnie.

"Right," Shawnie whispered back.

Funny hurried over. "Wow, you guys look great!"

"You mean, sensational!" Shawnie said, nudging Beth and grinning.

Funny laughed. "Yeah, and that, too. But the important question is, Are you ready for the show?"

Beth nodded. She felt pretty sure she could read her lines without looking at the paper. She had practiced saying the lines over and over again. The hard part would be looking directly into the camera when she was reading, and not looking away.

"I'm nervous," Beth admitted to Funny. "But I'm ready."

"Terrific," said Funny. "I know you'll be great."

Just then Paul walked into the media center wearing a blue pin-striped suit. He was carrying a small metal cage.

"He has Robin with him," observed Beth. "His mother must have dropped the bat off."

"Oh, good," Funny said, and hurried off to talk with Paul about his segment.

"Okay," Mr. Levine called out. "It's time. Everybody ready?"

"Ready!" Beth called back.

"Ready!" said Funny.

"Ready!" echoed Shane, who had just walked in with Tim.

"You don't *have* to be ready," Funny told him, giggling. "Your jobs are over for this week."

"We're here for moral support," explained Tim.

"Thanks, guys," said Beth. "We need it."

"Okay, let's get going," Mr. Levine said. "Beth and Shawnie, take your places."

Beth scurried over to their chairs and took out the teapot, setting it on the table. Shawnie had already set up the teacups and saucers.

"You guys aren't planning to drink anything during this show, are you?" Funny asked, eyeing the teacups doubtfully.

"No," Beth assured her. "They're just there for looks."

"For class," Shawnie added.

"Okay, good," Funny said, smiling. "The way you've dressed up the coffee table looks nice."

Mr. Levine turned to Funny. "Is the easel set up?"

"Yes." She dragged the easel that she'd borrowed from the art department over next to the set. On it, she placed a large posterboard sign with professionally printed letters that said, THE WAKEMAN BULLETIN BOARD.

"Good." Mr. Levine looked at it approvingly. "That's great."

"Okay, Jon," Funny said, "we'll come in on this sign first thing. We'll hear a couple of seconds of theme music, and then we'll shift the camera over to our co-anchors. Beth and Shawnie, when I begin to fade out the music, that's when you start the show. Okay?"

Beth and Shawnie nodded.

This is it, thought Beth. My big moment. *I'm really on TV!*

The red light on Jon's camera winked on, and Funny started the music. After a few seconds, she lowered the volume on the music, and Jon shifted the camera to the set, where Beth and Shawnie were sitting. Funny turned the volume down on the tape player again, and the music faded out completely.

"Good morning," Beth said, smiling into the camera. "Welcome to our first edition of *The Wakeman Bulletin Board.*"

"We'll be giving you important information on Wakeman activities," Shawnie said, "as well as reporting scores of your favorite sports teams and updating you on plans for school dances and performances."

"So get out your calendar," Beth said, "and be ready to write down some important dates."

A thrill ran up Beth's back. The show was going

well. No. It was going better than well. It was going terrifically, and she wasn't nervous anymore. And not only that, it was fun!

Beth thought about her new outfit and how perfect it made her look. Move over, Connie Chung, she thought. Beth glanced at Shawnie while Shawnie read the sports scores for the week. Shawnie had made a lot of this success possible.

Shawnie and her wonderful charge card!

CHAPTER

"**I**t went so well!" Beth burst out the instant she got home from the taping. "We didn't blow any lines, and Jon did a good job with the camera, and Paul Smoke had a great ecology segment."

"Fantastic!" Mrs. Barry said. "I'm so glad, honey. I know you worked hard on it and worried about it a lot."

"You bet. It's *The Wakeman Bulletin Board* today and the *Today* show tomorrow." Beth grinned broadly. Then she added silently, *By then I should have my own credit card!*

Her mother chuckled. "If you can come down off

cloud nine for a moment, you had a phone call from Mrs. Martin. She wants to know if you can baby-sit tomorrow. She has to pick up her sister at the airport."

"Great," said Beth. It was the answer to a prayer. She needed baby-sitting jobs to pay Shawnie back. "I'll call her right away."

Beth flipped through the phone book and quickly found the Martins' number.

"Mrs. Martin?" said Beth. "This is Beth Barry. Mom said you called about a baby-sitting job."

"That's right," Mrs. Martin answered. "Could you come tomorrow morning and stay with Jennifer and Davy from nine until eleven or so? Even though it's Saturday, my husband has to work and can't watch them."

Oh, no, Beth thought. I can't baby-sit then. The Fabulous Five are coming over for pancakes and to watch *The Wakeman Bulletin Board* on TV!

"Gosh, I'm sorry, Mrs. Martin," Beth said. "I can't come tomorrow. I've already made other plans."

"Okay." Mrs. Martin sounded disappointed. "I guess I'll have to try someone else."

Beth said good-bye and hung up. She stared out the window feeling guilty. She needed to take every baby-sitting job that came along if she was going to get Shawnie paid back any time soon. But she couldn't miss watching her own television debut! She crossed her fingers, hoping she would get another job offer before long.

"Mmm," said Jana. "Beth, these are the most delicious pancakes I've ever had."

"They sure are," agreed Melanie. "Can someone pass the syrup?"

"Mel, how can you eat all that syrup!" Christie said, making a face. "Your pancakes are already *swimming*!"

Melanie looked down at her plate. "They're not swimming. They're just treading water." She giggled. "I mean, treading syrup."

"What time is it?" asked Jana. "We can't miss your show."

"Are you kidding?" said Beth. "I've had one eye on the clock since I woke up this morning. It's exactly ten minutes to ten!"

"In ten minutes, Beth Barry—*our* Beth Barry—will become a TV star," declared Melanie. "I can't wait!"

Beth's mother poked her head in from the living room. "Beth, the time for your show is getting close. Dad is setting up the VCR to tape it."

Beth's five-year-old sister, Alicia, tore into the room and threw herself into Beth's arms, shrieking, "So we can watch it again and again and again and again and again and again—"

"All right, already!" Beth interrupted, laughing. She tickled Alicia until the little girl's words dissolved into a fit of giggles.

"Come on, you guys," Jana urged. "Let's get these dishes cleared so we're ready to sit down and watch the show."

The girls carried their dishes to the kitchen and hurried to the living room, where the rest of the Barry family was already sitting in front of the TV. Beth's mom and dad sat on the couch with Alicia perched on her mother's lap. Brittany sat cross-legged on the floor in front of Todd, who was sprawled out on a soft chair, and Brian, Beth's older brother, leaned against the door frame, nibbling a piece of toast. The volume was turned down so low, there was no sound coming from the TV.

"It's time," Beth said, flicking her eyes toward the mantel clock. "Turn up the sound, Jana."

Jana leaned forward and turned the volume switch. An instant later, the program began with a close-up of *The Wakeman Bulletin Board* sign. The theme music played in the background. Beth held her breath.

When the camera panned to Beth, there was a little gasp from everyone in the room. While Beth spoke on

TV, no one made a sound. But when the camera moved to Shawnie, Brittany turned and said, "Beth, you look really *great* on TV!"

"Yeah," Todd said, scratching his head, "what happened?"

Beth didn't even hear Todd because her head was spinning. She *did* look great! In fact, she looked almost better on TV than in person! The outfit she'd bought was *perfect*, and she looked like a pro in it. Her practicing the script had definitely paid off, too. She looked prepared and poised—just like Connie Chung.

The second the show was over, the room was filled with shouts of congratulations for Beth. Her friends and family had loved seeing her on TV.

The telephone rang, and Todd raced off to answer it.

"Hey, Beth," he said, returning a moment later. "Telephone. I think it's some guy named Keith." He grinned. "He probably wants to tell you how good you were."

"Hey, Beth, you were incredible!" Keith said when Beth picked up the receiver. "You really made Wakeman look good."

Beth's face turned red, and she was glad Keith couldn't see her.

"Thanks," she replied. "Everybody worked hard

this week. Did we look . . . well, you know, professional?"

"Totally!" Keith answered. "You guys were great."

A few minutes later Beth hung up with Keith. She felt so dizzy with happiness, she nearly floated back into the living room. Jana, Katie, Christie, and Melanie gathered around Beth while her family disappeared into other parts of the house.

"Everyone will be talking about this show at school on Monday!" Jana said.

"I can't wait to hear all the comments," Christie said.

"Your outfit looked terrific," added Melanie. "So what are you going to wear *next* Saturday?"

Beth stared at her friend a second. "Oh, my gosh," she mumbled. "I don't know. I didn't think past *this* show."

"Let's go shopping," suggested Melanie. "Right now. We'll help you find another great outfit."

Beth gulped. "I really do need something else to wear."

Jana looked doubtful. "I don't know, Beth. Even if we found something, how would you pay for it?"

Disappointment washed over Beth. "You're right, Jana," she said slowly. "I was so distracted I wasn't thinking. I can't possibly afford another outfit." Suddenly a glint appeared in her eye and she looked around the room at her friends. "There's no harm in looking though, is there?"

CHAPTER

7

"Ooh, guys," called Beth. She held up a blouse in a wild jungle print for her friends to see.

"That's really you," said Christie. "At least before you became a TV co-anchor."

"Right," said Jana. "You keep talking about more conservative clothes, like the kind you'd see Deborah Norville or Joan Lunden wearing."

"Oh, I know," admitted Beth. "Right now I'm interested in professional clothes. But I could just die for this jungle-print blouse to wear some other time. And maybe those earrings over there," she added, pointing to a mannequin wearing long earrings that were shaped like parrots. "They're perfect!"

Katie rolled her eyes. "You're a true shopaholic, Beth. You just love to buy clothes, period."

Beth laughed. "I can't deny it." She glanced slyly at her friends. "Let's go to Whitley's."

"*Whitley's?*" cried Jana. "I've never even been *in* that store! It's so expensive."

"We'll just go in for fun," Beth said. "We won't buy anything."

The others shrugged, and the five of them trooped through the mall to Whitley's. The salesclerk looked surprised to see them walk in.

"May I help you?" she asked doubtfully.

"We're just looking," Beth replied airily.

"I see," the woman said, but she kept watching them.

Beth looked all through their smallest sizes. The styles were gorgeous, but a bit too mature for her.

"I don't see anything here," Beth said to the others. "Let's go."

They headed for the door.

"Hey, look at this stuff!" Melanie exclaimed.

Beth noticed the salesclerk frown. She probably didn't like to hear Whitley's merchandise described as "stuff."

Melanie was standing over a small table of discounted jewelry and accessory items. "What a great scarf!" she said, holding up the filmy material in shades of blue and purple.

"Wow," Beth said. She took the scarf from Melanie and hurried to a nearby three-way mirror. Draping it over her shoulder, she struck a dramatic pose.

"Isn't it *di-vine?*"

The salesclerk rushed over. "May I *help* you?"

Beth gazed at the woman. *She thinks I'm going to wreck this scarf,* she thought. She whipped the scarf off and found the price tag. Even on sale, it was very expensive.

"I'm interested in this scarf," Beth said to the clerk.

"It's beautiful," Melanie said. "You could wear it around your neck or shoulders."

"It would look terrific with your blue dress," Christie suggested. "You could even wear it on TV."

"That's right," Beth said slowly. "And it would be a lot cheaper than buying a whole new outfit."

"May I wrap it up, then?" the woman asked curtly.

It was very expensive, but Beth was annoyed at the clerk's attitude. She had as much right to shop in this store as anyone else! *That clerk wouldn't treat Connie Chung this way,* Beth thought. *Or Barbara Walters.* She giggled at the thought.

"I'll take it," she said, handing it to the clerk.

"Very well," the clerk said, taking the scarf. She turned and headed up to the cash register.

"How are you going to pay for it?" Jana whispered to Beth.

Beth stared at her friend, and her mouth dropped open. "*Oh, my gosh!*" she said. "I got carried away! I have less than *half* the price with me, not counting the tax!"

"You really want the scarf, don't you?" Jana asked.

"Yes," Beth admitted, "but I have to put it back."

Jana opened her purse. "I have some money."

"I can't take your money," Beth insisted.

"I can contribute some," volunteered Christie.

"Me, too," Katie chimed in.

"Hey, when you're famous," Melanie said, "I can say I lent you some money for your first TV series."

Beth grinned. "Thanks, you guys. This is my last purchase for the show. I promise I'll pay you back as soon as I can."

The girls pooled all of their money and came up with just eleven cents over the price of the scarf plus tax.

"*Young ladies,*" the salesclerk said impatiently from the cash register, "are you ready?"

"Of course," Beth said triumphantly. She strode up

to the cash register and, with a flourish, handed her the money. "It's all there."

When The Fabulous Five left Whitley's they walked down half the corridor before any of them spoke.

"That lady was just too much," Beth said.

"What a snob!" agreed Christie.

Melanie chuckled. "Maybe you should have told her to watch *The Wakeman Bulletin Board* on Saturday and see her precious scarf on TV."

Beth took out the scarf and unwrapped it from the tissue paper. She took a corner and let the scarf unfold itself, then draped it over her arm. "It's really beautiful."

"It sure is," Jana replied.

Beth looked up gratefully at her friends. "Thank you," she said softly. "You four are the best friends I could ever have."

"Wow, you looked great on TV!" Dekeisha Adams called out to Beth when she walked into the school building Monday morning.

Pam Wolthoff waved to Beth from her locker. "Hey, TV star! You were terrific!"

Another girl called out, "Beth, you were really cool on *The Wakeman Bulletin Board*. Great job!"

All day, in each of her classes, people came up to Beth to congratulate her on how well she had done on the cable show. It felt *wonderful* to be recognized for doing a good job, and even for looking good while she was doing it.

That Monday during school was certainly one of the best days Beth could ever remember. She felt like a celebrity.

"Hey, Beth," Shawnie said, catching up with her at her locker after school before the Media Club meeting. "Have you decided what you're going to wear during Friday's shoot?"

"No," Beth replied, tossing her math book into her locker. "I haven't."

Just then ninth-grader Andy Trudeau walked past and gave Shawnie's arm a squeeze. "You guys looked great on TV. Keep up the good work."

Shawnie beamed at him. "Thanks, Andy. Beth," she whispered as he walked away, "everybody keeps telling us that we looked great. We *have* to wear coordinating outfits again. Do you think you could convince your parents to let you get something new?"

"No way," Beth said. "I couldn't get them to buy me a new outfit last week."

"Well." Shawnie sighed. "We'll just have to go to Tanninger's and use my credit card again."

Beth shook her head. "I don't think so. Everything at Tanninger's is so expensive and I already owe you and my friends in The Fabulous Five money."

"Look," Shawnie said. "Let's go over there after the Media Club meeting today and see what's on sale. They always have a sale rack."

Beth hesitated, thinking about how wonderful it was to hear how great she looked on TV. "Okay, Shawnie," Beth said finally. "Let's see what's on sale."

"Great," cried Shawnie. "I'll see you in a few minutes at the meeting."

As Shawnie hurried down the hall, Beth closed her locker door and leaned her head against it. "How do I get myself into these messes?" she murmured to herself.

On Saturday she had told her friends she would wear the new scarf with her blue dress for the taping. But now after all the compliments she'd received today, she wasn't so sure the scarf was good enough.

"Face it, Beth Barry. Katie was absolutely right— you're a hopeless *shopaholic*!"

She turned and trudged down the hall toward the media center.

CHAPTER

*M*r. Levine called the meeting of the Media Club to order. "From the comments I've heard today, *The Wakeman Bulletin Board* program on Saturday was an unqualified hit."

"Was it ever!" cried Funny. "It's all the kids were talking about all day."

"Yeah," said Jon, "and mostly they were talking about how great Beth and Shawnie were."

Mr. Levine nodded. "I'll agree with that. Beth and Shawnie, you both did an excellent job. You looked like real pros in front of the camera. But, of course, *all* of you did a terrific job. Our co-anchors were more visible than any of you others, so I'm not surprised that they received the lion's share of the compliments. But I'm proud of each and every one of you."

Everyone in the room seemed to beam in response to Mr. Levine's praise. Beth watched her fellow club members' faces and felt a warm glow. Mr. Levine had said she looked like a pro in front of the camera. That was the biggest compliment he could give her.

"Everyone is expecting us to be really good again," said Funny, "so we can't sit back on our laurels. Let's make our next show even better."

"Right!" exclaimed Paul.

"You will all keep your jobs for the rest of the month," Mr. Levine reminded them. "Tim and Shane, we'll need your information by Wednesday again so Funny can write the script. Paul, your bat presentation was great, and very interesting. But we'll need something different for the ecology segment this week. Have any ideas?"

Paul shrugged. "I've been thinking about it," he said. "How about doing something on recycling?"

"Sounds good so far," Funny spoke up. "What did you have in mind?"

"Well," said Paul, "we could remind the kids that it's important to save cans, bottles, newspapers, and stuff like that. And tell them where the recycling companies and drop-off boxes are located around town."

Shane made a face. "You see a lot of that kind of information in the newspapers. Maybe we could do something more original."

"Like what?" asked Paul.

Nobody had any ideas.

"I guess I'll just have to keep thinking," Paul said. "And if anybody comes up with any good ideas, please *see me*!"

"Hey, that's what we're here for." Funny grinned. "To help one another."

Funny was right, Beth thought. That's what had made this project so much fun and the show so good. Surely someone would come up with an idea for Paul before the taping on Friday. No one would want to see the ecology segment turn into a disaster. She gulped and glanced at Shawnie. Without her help and her plastic card, *I* would have been a disaster.

"And speaking of helping one another," Mr. Levine said, "Shane has some relatives visiting, so he won't have time to make posters advertising this week's show."

"Hey, are Igor's cousins coming over?" Tim teased.

Everybody laughed, and Mr. Levine held up his

hand for quiet. "Would any of you have time to do, say, *one* poster?"

Jon raised his hand. "Anything for Igor and his cousins."

"I'll make one, too," offered Beth.

"Thanks, guys," Shane said. "Igor and I owe you one."

"Good," said Mr. Levine. "With the ones Tim will make, we should have enough."

When the meeting broke up, Beth left the media center feeling confident that the show would be really good again. If only she could get something decent to wear.

Beth and Shawnie spent half an hour in the juniors department at Tanninger's before Beth found something she loved that was on sale. She stood in front of the mirror in the small dressing room and turned to the right and to the left. Instead of the scarf, she would wear this terrific navy blazer over her blue dress.

"I would have never believed that I—*Beth Barry*—would ever buy something as conservative as a navy blue blazer," she said, shaking her head in amazement, "but this one is perfect!" Her smile faded a little. "Honestly, though, Shawnie, this will be the very *last* thing I buy. And I'll start paying your parents back right away. I promise!"

Shawnie dismissed the idea with a wave of her hand. "Beth, the blazer really is gorgeous. And think about it this way—you didn't buy a *whole* new outfit, right? You're going to wear it with a dress you already have, and it was on sale."

Beth nodded. It all sounded so reasonable when Shawnie put it that way.

Beth turned again to her reflection and smiled. She was going to look classy again. She couldn't wait for Friday's taping.

Beth pried off the top of the paint can. The paint was bright red, perfect for the poster.

She had carefully lettered the sign in hollow block letters.

WATCH THE WAKEMAN BULLETIN BOARD
ON THE
SPECTRUM CHANNEL, SATURDAY, 10 A.M.
DON'T MISS OUT!
ALL YOUR FRIENDS WILL BE WATCHING!

She picked up the wooden stirring stick lying on the newspaper, dipped it into the paint, and began to stir. She glanced around at her father's basement workshop. What an amazing assortment of stuff! Tools hung on the pegboard over the workbench, Alicia's old high chair stood in the corner with a plastic sheet covering it, a box of wood scraps was pushed up against the far wall, and her dad's fishing gear sat at the side of the workbench.

It wasn't exactly tidy. The work area was strewn with odd screws and bolts, and a short piece of fishing line was lying next to the paint can.

Beth leaned over and picked up the line to move it away from her work area, but it slipped from her fingers and dropped into the red paint. Letting out a disgusted sigh, she dipped her fingers into the paint to retrieve the line.

"Yuck," she muttered. "It's a good thing this paint is washable. Painted nails are one thing, but who needs painted fingers?"

She dropped the wet fishing line on the newspaper to take care of later. Then she wiped the paint off her hands with a rag, took a small brush, dipped it into the paint, and began filling in the letters on her poster.

When she finished nearly an hour later, she pushed the lid back onto the paint can and began to clean up. The red fishing line caught her eye. It was dry now, and Beth picked it up, dangling it by two fingers. It was such a pretty bright red. She almost hated to throw it away.

An idea leapt into Beth's mind. *If I cut the string in two pieces . . .*

She reached for a heavy pair of scissors on the work-table and snipped the piece of line in two. She took one of the pieces, which was now about four inches long, and put the two ends together so that the middle looped down.

If I attached the ends to earring backs, she thought, they'd make a super pair of new earrings. Then an-other idea hit her. Maybe she could string buttons or beads on the line. She was sure she could find some in her mother's jar of extras.

Beth quickly finished cleaning up and then went back inside the house, carrying the fishing line. In her mother's sewing basket she found two red, white, and blue buttons attached to a card that had originally held eight buttons.

"All right," she said happily as she threaded each piece of line through the holes in one of the buttons. Next she hurried to the jewelry box in her room and took out the earring posts and backs she had stashed there a year ago when she'd bought a tiny package of them to repair some earrings that she'd broken. Next, she got out the jewelry glue and went to work.

Stepping up to her mirror a little while later, she held the new earrings up to her ears. "Fantastic!" she cried. "Jewelry from junk." She grinned at her reflection. "Beth Barry, you're a genius. Wait till everyone sees your new earrings tomorrow." Then she added ruefully, "The best thing about them is that they didn't cost a cent!"

CHAPTER

"It's serendipity!" Christie exclaimed.

"What kind of *dipity*?" asked Beth.

"Serendipity," her friend repeated. "It's when you make a wonderful discovery by accident."

"Well, whatever it's called, those earrings are terrific," said Melanie.

The Fabulous Five had gathered at their meeting spot by the fence before school the next day. Beth was wearing her new creations.

"I can't believe that you made such great earrings with nothing but junk from around the house," said Jana.

"Right," agreed Katie. "I wish I had a pair."

"I'll make you some," Beth offered.

"Really?" said Katie.

"Sure, I'll make each of you a pair," Beth promised. "Not only that, each pair will be an exclusive, one-of-a-kind design. Something that will fit your personality."

Melanie beamed. "Can you make mine in the shape of hearts?"

"No problem," Beth replied.

Just then the bell rang, and the girls went into the building and separated to go to their classes.

Dekeisha Adams smiled and waved as Beth passed her locker. Then Dekeisha did a double take.

"Hey, Beth!" she called out. "Wait a minute. Where did you get those awesome earrings?"

"I made them," Beth said, "by accident."

Dekeisha cocked an eyebrow. "By accident?"

"Yup," said Beth.

"So what are they made of?" Dekeisha asked. "I mean, besides the buttons?"

Beth laughed. "Would you believe fishing line and red paint?"

Dekeisha laughed, too. "Wow. I love them."

"Thanks," Beth said, and hurried on down the hall. By the time Beth got to her first-period class, five people had stopped her to ask about her earrings. But

more than that, she had come up with a terrific idea for
The Wakeman Bulletin Board.

After school she hurried to her locker to put away
her books. The Media Club was meeting in five minutes, and she could hardly wait to tell everyone her
great idea. She was shoving her books onto the top
shelf when she felt a tug on her hair. She whirled
around.

"Keith! What do you think you're doing?"

Keith shrugged and slumped against her locker.
"Pulling your hair."

"There's not much to pull," she said with a laugh,
looking up into his eyes. He was so cute. His blondish
hair was swept back a little from his forehead, and his
eyes were twinkling as he gazed back at her.

"I haven't seen much of you since your awesome appearance on TV," he said.

"I know," she said. "I've been pretty busy with the
Media Club."

He reached out and touched one of her earrings.
"Hey, these are great. Are they new?"

Beth grinned. "Yes and no."

"What's that supposed to mean?" Keith asked.

"They're brand-new earrings made out of old junk I
found around the house."

Keith looked impressed. "Wow! You're not only pretty and talented, but artistic, too."

Beth felt her cheeks heat up. "Thanks."

"What are you doing after the Media Club meeting?" he asked. "Want to meet me at Bumpers?"

"Sure," she replied. "Our meeting should be over in about an hour. I'll see you then."

Beth watched Keith walk down the hall and out the door. He had seemed so proud of her TV appearance. She hoped she could be as successful on this week's show.

Shawnie let out a whoop when she saw Beth's earrings.

"Hey," she exclaimed. "These are wonderful."

Funny, Paul, and Shane walked over just as Shawnie moved in close to examine the earrings. Then she stood back and narrowed her eyes, deep in thought.

"You got them at the Treasure Trove, right?" Shawnie asked.

Beth smiled and shook her head. Shawnie knew the mall better than any other living human.

"Don't tell me, don't tell me," Shawnie insisted, waving her hands. "Let me think. I know! Emerson's."

"Nope."

"Hmmm," Shawnie said. "Juniors' Jungle?"

"No," Funny interjected. "I'd guess Earrings Galore."

Beth laughed. "I didn't buy them anywhere. I *made* them."

Shawnie gave her a skeptical look. "Aw, come on."

"I'm perfectly serious," Beth insisted. "Not only that, I made them out of stuff I found around the house, which means that they're recycled junk." She turned to Paul. "Are you still looking for ideas for your ecology segment? I could bring them to the taping and show the audience how to make something out of nothing."

"Beth, you're a genius!" Paul exclaimed. "That's just exactly the kind of thing we're looking for. Can you make more? You know, different styles?"

"Sure," said Beth.

"That's a super idea," said Funny.

"I think so, too," agreed Mr. Levine. "It would be a great addition to the show. I think the kids will be very interested to learn how you make them."

"I'll do it," Beth said, grinning. Then she laughed and struck a dramatic pose. "Anything for the cause!"

When Beth walked through the door of Bumpers, she saw Keith sitting in a booth with Randy Kirwan and Jana. Keith waved as soon as he saw her.

She hurried over to join them.

"What'll you have?" Keith asked.

"Something big, and gooey, and chocolate," said Beth, rubbing her hands together in anticipation.

Keith started scooting out of the booth to head for the order counter when Shawnie came rushing up.

"Beth!" she said, breathlessly. "I forgot to tell you— I was distracted by your earrings at the meeting. My parents will kill me if I don't give you this message." Shawnie ran her finger across her throat and made a cutting sound. "They say you *have* to start paying them back for your purchases right away."

Beth's heart started beating hard. She felt her cheeks flame. She had never been so mortified in her life. And why hadn't Shawnie talked to her in private instead of in front of Keith and Jana and Randy?

"Right away?" she murmured.

Shawnie nodded. "My parents weren't thrilled that I loaned you my card. They want the money for what you charged by the time the bill comes in. They don't want to have to lay out the money themselves."

Beth couldn't look up, so she just nodded stiffly, knowing everyone could see how humiliated she was. "Of course." Her voice was soft. "I'll start paying them back this weekend when I get my allowance. Tell them they can expect my first payment then."

Shawnie shook her head. "I don't think that your allowance will be enough, Beth," she said. "My parents want you to pay at least thirty percent of what you owe. If you pay that much each week, it will all be paid off by the time the bill comes in."

Beth jerked herself upright. "Thirty percent!" She did some quick figuring in her head and gasped. "Shawnie, my allowance isn't even *ten* percent!"

Shawnie frowned. "I'm sorry, Beth, but my parents are pretty steamed at me for letting you use my credit card."

Beth felt as if she were sinking in quicksand. "Well . . . maybe I can drum up some baby-sitting jobs this weekend," she said hopefully.

"I'm supposed to pick up your payment on Friday after the shoot," Shawnie told her.

"*Oh, no!*" cried Beth. It felt as if a rock had suddenly formed in her stomach.

Shawnie nodded. "Or they say they'll call your parents."

Beth groaned and slumped back against the booth. The rock had just turned to a boulder.

"My parents are going to be furious!" She held her head in her hands, no longer worried about being embarrassed in front of her friends. "I should *never* have bought those things!"

She felt a hand on her arm. "Beth," Jana said softly. "I could lend you—"

Beth felt a tingle of hope for an instant, but then she

shook her head and said emphatically, "No! That's what got me into this mess in the first place. Borrowing money and buying on credit!" She looked at Jana, and her face softened. "Thanks, Jana, but I'm going to have to get myself out of this." Then she looked at Shawnie again. "Tell your parents that I'll talk with my mom and dad, and that they will be paid back as quickly as possible."

"Okay," said Shawnie. She turned and left Bumpers.

"I don't know what that was all about," Keith began, "but if you need some help—"

Beth rose from the table. "It's my mess and something I'm going to have to take care of." She looked at the floor, feeling embarrassed and a little sick to her stomach all over again. "I'm really sorry to run off like this, but I don't think I'd be very good company right now."

"No problem," Randy said.

"I'll talk to you later," Keith said. He reached over and squeezed Beth's hand.

"Thanks," she said to all of them.

"I'll call you tonight," Jana said. "Good luck."

Beth sighed. "I'm going to need as much of that as I can get."

She gathered up her book bag and slung it over her shoulder. Then she and the boulder in her stomach headed out the door toward home.

CHAPTER

10

"*H*ow in the world am I going to tell them?" Beth whispered. She had stopped outside Bumpers and was trying to hear herself think above the pounding of her heart. She couldn't just go home and admit to her parents that she had gone behind their backs and run up a bill for new clothes that they had told her she definitely could not have because money was tight right now. And she certainly couldn't tell them the truth about sneaking out to the mall with Shawnie and then lying to them by saying that Shawnie had lent her the outfits.

"I didn't lie," she corrected herself as she headed

slowly in the direction of home. "I never *ever* said that Shawnie lent me the clothes." She swallowed hard at the thought of what she had actually said. "I just put it in a way that made them think she did."

Scuffing along, she wished desperately that something—*anything*—would come along and make the whole problem disappear.

Maybe her parents had entered a million-dollar sweepstakes, and the letter would come today saying they had won. Then the amount she had charged at Tanninger's would hardly mean a thing.

Or maybe her father had just gotten a humongous promotion and raise, and to celebrate he would give each of the Barry kids a crisp, new one-hundred-dollar bill!

"Dream on," Beth muttered, and kicked a rock into the street.

When she got home, she tiptoed up to her room. I'm not really stalling, Beth told herself. I'm just not ready. She racked her brain. How could she explain it so that her parents would understand? Nothing she could think of sounded right.

Talking to them at dinner was out of the question. Todd and Alicia were squabbling over whose turn it was to clear the table. Brian was telling Mr. Barry about a hot new car one of his friends had, and Brittany was listening for the phone, as usual. For once in her life, Beth was glad she was the middle child. The one no one ever paid any attention to. That way, no one noticed that she only picked at her food as she agonized over her impending moment of doom.

As soon as dinner was over, she hurried back to her room to try one more time to find the perfect thing to say.

"You see, Mom and Dad, Shawnie practically *forced* me to use her credit card. And she said her parents wouldn't *care* and that I could take *forever* to pay her back."

Beth sighed. Of course, that wasn't exactly true. Shawnie hadn't forced her to do anything. On the other hand, Beth argued with herself, Shawnie did insist, saying that I had to look good enough to be on the show with her. Beth bristled at the thought. It really was partly Shawnie's fault. If she hadn't been so worried that I'd wear something awful and embarrass her, probably none of this would ever have happened.

And Shawnie *did* say that her parents wouldn't care. And that I could take *as long as I wanted* to pay her back. So it *is* partly her fault, after all.

Beth flopped onto her bed and stared at the ceiling. But what good would it do to blame Shawnie? Her own parents would say it didn't make any difference. That she knew the rules in the Barry family and she had broken them. Besides, Beth thought, Shawnie's never had to worry about money, so she doesn't understand what it's like in a family that does. She wasn't trying to get me in trouble on purpose.

Suddenly Beth sat up with a start. What if she talked to Shawnie's parents instead of her own? After all, they were rich and didn't really need the money, anyway. She could phone them and explain that she couldn't possibly pay thirty percent by Friday, and maybe they could work out a payment plan to last for the next year or so. That way she *could* pay the Pendergasts back, and her own parents would never have to know or be disappointed in her. Maybe she could even work off part of the debt, doing chores for Mr. and Mrs. Pendergast. She'd do anything. It would be worth it. She'd be their slave.

Slumping back against her pillow, she closed her eyes and thought about Shawnie's parents. It was easy to see where Shawnie got her good looks. They were both tall and thin and very expensive-looking, with an air about them that they were always busy. Terribly busy. Almost too busy to breathe. That wasn't all. Every time she'd been around them, Beth had had another feeling about them. They were crabby. And unsympathetic. That's why they gave Shawnie credit cards instead of love.

Beth swallowed the lump in her throat. At least her own parents loved her. Even when she did something totally stupid like this. And even though they couldn't buy her lots of expensive clothes or give her her own credit card, she would a million, billion, zillion, *lillion* times rather talk to them than to Shawnie's parents. And she would do it right now, she thought with determination.

Beth blew her nose and stuck a couple of extra tissues into her jeans pocket. Then, crossing and uncrossing her fingers three times for luck, she headed down the stairs to find her mom and dad.

CHAPTER

11

"You did what!" Mr. Barry exploded over the top of the sports page. He leaned forward, pushing his recliner into an upright position, and gave Beth an astonished stare.

Her mother was frowning as she put the mystery she was reading down on the sofa beside her. "I think you'd better explain."

Beth nodded. She wasn't sure she could. The lump in her throat was getting bigger by the second. But she took a deep breath and started telling her parents all about using Shawnie's credit card to get new clothes to wear on TV.

As soon as Beth finished, she could see that her parents looked just as angry and disappointed with her as she had expected them to be.

"This is very serious, Beth," Mrs. Barry said finally. "I hope you understand that."

"I do," Beth answered in a small voice.

"I simply can't believe you'd do it!" Mr. Barry looked at her, shaking his head. "You sneaked around. You lied . . ." His voice trailed off in exasperation.

Beth hung her head. "I know. I just got carried away."

"Well, young lady," her father said, "I think your mother and I had better talk this situation over. Go up to your room, and we'll be up to discuss this further in a little while. Why don't you give some thought to solutions, too."

Beth dragged herself up the stairs. What could she do? She didn't have any money stashed anywhere. There was only one solution. Her parents would have to pay the Pendergasts' credit card bill, and then she would have to spend the rest of her life paying her parents back.

In her room she went to her closet and pulled out the gorgeous black dress with the red trim she had worn last week. She held it up and looked at herself sadly in the mirror. If only she had never seen this beautiful dress. Or, at the very least, resisted the temptation to buy it. With a sigh she hung it back in the closet. As she started to step back, her gaze fell on the blazer hanging next to it. The great blue blazer she planned to wear for Friday's taping. It had never been worn. In fact, the tags were still on it.

Beth bit her bottom lip. She didn't *absolutely* have to have the blazer. Her old dress would look brand-new with the scarf from Whitley's. And if she took the blazer back to Tanninger's and asked them to credit Shawnie's account with the purchase price, that would make up for some of what she owed.

She was feeling a little better by the time her parents knocked on her bedroom door a few minutes later, and she eagerly explained her plan to return the unworn blazer.

"That's a wonderful idea," her father said, sounding genuinely pleased.

"The next order of business is to decide how you will pay off the Pendergasts' credit card bill," said her mother.

"I know," Beth whispered.

"We'll take care of their payment," said Mr. Barry, "but then you'll have to pay us back."

"And take care of the debt you incurred with your friends," added her mother.

"We've decided that your allowance will come directly back to us, and every penny you earn baby-sitting will come to us until your debt is paid off," said her father.

"Okay," Beth agreed. "That sounds fair."

"It's *more* than fair," said her mother. "When you're out on your own, there won't be anyone to bail you out of trouble, you know."

"That's right," added her father. "People can lose everything they've worked for if they get into debt over their heads."

Beth nodded. "I know. I've learned my lesson."

"Honey," Mrs. Barry said, "I think we need to re-think some of your spending habits. Would you get us some paper and a pencil."

Beth got up and grabbed a pad and pencil.

"Let's write down how much you usually spend in a week and see how you're spending it," her mother continued.

"Okay." Beth thought a minute. "Well, there are sodas and ice cream and sometimes french fries at Bumpers a couple of afternoons a week, paperbacks at the bookstore"— she glanced at her mother, who was busily writing what she said, along with approximately how much those items cost —"and maybe a pair of earrings or a necklace or something when I go to the mall on Saturdays. Oh, and tapes and records, too."

"And you buy your lunch at the mall, too, right?" her mother said.

"Yeah, and sometimes we go to a movie."

Her mother held her pencil poised over the list. "Is that it?"

"I guess. That's kind of an average week."

"Okay," her mother said. "Let's add those up." She did the figuring and showed the total to Beth and her father. "Now let's write down your allowance."

"They're almost the same amount," Beth said sadly.

Mrs. Barry nodded. "That's right. Now, you have baby-sitting jobs that allow you to buy a little extra occasionally."

"A lot of times I save baby-sitting money to buy birthday and Christmas presents," Beth pointed out.

Mrs. Barry looked at her husband. "What do you think, dear?"

"I think it's time for Beth to start a savings program," he said, turning to Beth.

Her mother nodded. "After you pay off your debt to the Pendergasts and your friends, we'd like you to begin saving half of everything you earn."

Beth's heart sank. "*Half?*" she whispered in astonishment.

"You know, Beth, college isn't many years away," her mother said. "With five kids, your dad and I will need for you to help out with college expenses."

"But . . ." Beth interjected.

Her mother held up her hand. "If you start saving half of what you earn now, you'll have a substantial amount of money when you *really* need it," she went on.

Beth had expected a lecture on finances. She knew that what her parents were saying was absolutely true, but that didn't make it any easier to sit here and listen to it. And putting *half* her money into a savings account sounded horrible! How could she possibly do that?

"But Mom, Dad," she said in her most controlled voice. "If I have to save half of what I earn, I'll only be able to buy *half* the number of sodas, I probably won't be able to afford a new pair of earrings, and there's no way I'll be able to go to a movie, no matter how super it is . . . or how *educational*," she added, hoping to tip the scale.

"Well," said Mr. Barry, and Beth saw a twinkle in his eye as he looked at her mother, "I think that if we require you to save half of what you earn, it's appropriate that we increase your allowance a bit."

Beth brightened. "Really?" she said. She wondered

how much "a bit" was, but she knew this was definitely *not* the time to ask!

"Really," her dad answered. Then he pointed at her. "But we expect you to watch your money and your spending more carefully from now on."

"I will," Beth said sincerely. "I don't ever want to get into this mess again!" She shivered.

"Good," said her mother.

Beth sighed with relief. Her talk with her parents hadn't been fun, but it could have been worse. Much worse. After all, she wasn't grounded until she was twenty-one or anything.

But it was going to take a very long time—*months!*—to pay off her parents, and during that time, she wouldn't be able to order snacks at Bumpers or go shopping with her friends at the mall, or go to the movies, or—oh, it seemed too awful to think about.

Beth put her face in her hands, and her mother stroked her hair. "You're going to have a tough couple of months, honey," her mother said. Beth looked up at her and smiled a little. "But you'll live."

Beth groaned and put her face back down into her hands.

Maybe, she thought. Just maybe.

CHAPTER

*P*aul finished his part of the ecology segment and smiled into the camera. "And now Beth Barry will share an idea with you for making something out of practically nothing. I think you're going to like this!"

Jon shifted the camera to Beth. She looked into the lens and smiled.

"I have something exciting to show you this morning," she said. "It's distinctive and attractive, and it makes a definite fashion statement. I call it Junque Jewelry. Jon, can we get a close-up of this?"

Beth saw Jon tilt the camera down to focus on the

jewelry items with the little sign she'd made saying JUNQUE JEWELRY behind them.

She was proud of how her creations looked. She had spent the rest of the week working on them, and now her jewelry was displayed on top of a board she had covered with blue velvet. The jewelry shone and glistened under the bright TV lights.

Beth centered the board in front of her and pointed to each item. "This pair of earrings was made from fishing line, paint, and colorful buttons." She slid her hand along the display. "This pair was made of thin wire and a couple of bus tokens. I used old luggage keys to make the next pair."

Then she pointed to the other side of the blue velvet tray, where some of her more unusual creations were. "To make this necklace, I tied a lot of knots and loops in a long piece of fishing line and then sprayed it with gold paint," she continued. "For the matching earrings, I used shorter line and fewer tangles."

Out of the corner of her eye Beth could see admiring glances from Funny and Shawnie. They seemed to really like her jewelry.

Beth pointed to the last item on the tray. "I made this necklace by cutting out the individual circles from a plastic six-pack holder and painting each circle a different color. Then I strung them together. You can use the individual circles from the six-pack holder for earrings, too."

Beth looked up into the camera. "The best thing about Junque Jewelry is that it's unique *and* you can make it from whatever you find around the house. All it takes is a little imagination!" She looked to her left. "Shawnie?"

Jon shifted the video camera back to Shawnie, who was dressed in a stunning ice-blue suit. A large ribbon of the same shade of blue held back her hair. With a tiny stab of jealousy, Beth thought about the gorgeous blue blazer she'd returned to Tanninger's. It was true that she'd like to be wearing the blazer, but she really didn't need it. Actually, her old blue dress and the new scarf from Whitley's looked great together.

Shawnie continued the program by reporting the lunch menus for next week. Beth noticed that she wrinkled her nose ever so slightly when she mentioned the goulash. Beth almost laughed out loud. Everybody hated the school's goulash!

After the taping was finished, everyone agreed that the show was even better than it had been the week before.

"Beth," Funny said, "I think your Junque Jewelry was the hit of the show."

"I agree," said Mr. Levine. "Viewers should be very interested in that segment. Good work."

"Thanks," replied Beth. She thought it had gone well and was pleased that the others agreed.

As the members of the Media Club began packing up their belongings and taking down the lights, Shawnie approached Beth and guided her out into the hall.

"Sorry about this, Beth," she said. "But my parents reminded me this morning that I have to collect that thirty percent from you today."

Beth nodded. She unzipped her book bag and pulled out a check. "Here it is," she said, "minus the price of the blue blazer, which I took back and had credited to your account." She handed the check to Shawnie.

Shawnie glanced down at the check. "It's from your parents," she murmured. "You really told them? I didn't think you'd actually do it."

"Yup," Beth replied. "I finally told them what was going on. They wanted to pay your parents back right away, and so I'll pay *them* back."

"Wow. Were they furious?" Shawnie asked.

Beth shrugged. "They weren't thrilled, but in the end they were pretty nice about it."

"How long will it take you to pay them back?" asked Shawnie.

Beth sighed. "I don't know. But it will probably be a while before I make any trips to the mall."

Shawnie nodded and was silent for a minute. Then

she said, "We really knocked 'em dead again today. And you know what?"

"What?" asked Beth.

"Your blue dress looks even better with just the scarf than it would have if you'd been wearing that blazer," Shawnie said. "But that's not all. You've got poise and imagination." She paused a moment. "That's even more important than looking stupendous."

"Thanks, Shawnie." Beth grinned. "It was an expensive lesson, but I guess I just learned that."

CHAPTER

13

"This pair with the buttons is for you." Beth handed the earrings to Jana.

"Oh, Beth," Jana exclaimed. "I love them."

"And these with the bus tokens are for you, Christie," Beth said.

Christie laughed. "They're great! What a conversation piece."

It was Saturday morning, and the girls were lounging on Beth's front porch, waiting to watch *The Wakeman Bulletin Board*.

"The earrings with the multicolored paper clips are yours, Katie," Beth said.

"When I'm not wearing them, I can clip together my notes for Teen Court," Katie joked. "Thanks."

"And these little key earrings go to Melanie." Beth grinned. "I'll bet you can guess the significance of these."

"The key to my heart!" Melanie said. "Thanks."

"But there are two of them," Jana pointed out.

"Of course," Beth insisted. "Have you ever known Melanie to stick to only *one* boy at a time?"

Melanie giggled. "Maybe you should add a couple more keys—just in case."

"How about a whole key ring on each ear?" Katie joked.

Laughter filled the porch.

"Thanks, Beth," Jana said. "These earrings are so great. I just love them."

The others chimed in their thanks again, too.

"You're welcome," Beth replied as she sat back in the porch swing, tucking one leg up underneath her.

"So you can't go to Bumpers until you pay off the loan from your parents?" Jana asked.

"Well, I can *go*," said Beth. "But I won't have any money to buy anything. I'll just watch you guys eat."

"It probably won't be so bad," remarked Jana.

Beth sighed. "Yeah, I know. It'll just be hard to get

used to it. No movies, no shopping, no treats, no—
anything!"

Melanie shrugged. "You still have *us*."

Beth smiled. "You're right about that, Mel. I still
have you guys!"

The front door opened, and a little face peered out.

"Bethy," Alicia said, "Mommy says it's almost time
for your show to be on."

"Okay. Thanks," Beth said.

The girls trooped inside and plopped down on the
floor in front of the TV. The rest of the Barry family
was there.

"Yeah, well, let's see if you can top *last* week's show,"
challenged Todd.

"Of course I can!" Beth said, accepting his chal-
lenge. "We're even *better* this week."

"I'll be the judge of that," Todd muttered, turning to
face the television.

Beth stuck her tongue out at Todd's back, and the
rest of The Fabulous Five laughed.

Just then the sign for *The Wakeman Bulletin Board* appeared on the screen, and Beth scooted forward and
turned up the volume.

"Shh," she said. "Here it is."

For the next few minutes everyone in the room

quietly watched the cable show. When Beth's Junque Jewelry segment came on, the girls sat forward.

"Hey, there are my earrings!" Jana exclaimed, watching Beth's hand on the screen point to the pair with the buttons.

"And mine!" said Christie, eyeing the pair with the bus tokens.

"And there are the keys to my heart!" Melanie cried, clapping her hands.

"The keys to your heart?" Todd said. He and Brian looked at each other and rolled their eyes.

When the camera went back to Shawnie, Beth turned to Katie. "Sorry," she said. "I didn't get yours made until last night."

"No problem," Katie answered, waving her hand.

As Beth watched the show, she felt as proud this week as she had the week before. The show really was good, and her Junque Jewelry looked fabulous on TV! It was definitely a super addition to the ecology portion of the show.

She also couldn't help thinking that she looked just fine in her old blue dress. It was great to wear new, expensive clothes, of course, but what really made the show special was the professionalism of the whole team. The information presented was interesting, the camera work was smooth, and the whole production was organized and well rehearsed. Why hadn't she seen how much that mattered before she'd spent all that money to look good? Why hadn't she realized that it wasn't her wardrobe that would make her become another Joan Lunden or Connie Chung someday?

When the show ended, Katie turned to Todd. "Okay. You have to agree that Beth's Junque Jewelry was the hit of the show, and this show was better than the first one."

Brittany socked Todd in the arm. "Admit it, Todd. It *was* better."

"It was terrific," said Brian. "Even with you in it, Beth."

"*Especially* with Bethy in it!" Alicia cried.

"You tell 'em, Alicia." Mrs. Barry laughed.

Beth turned to Todd. "*Better* than last week, right?" Todd tried not to smile. "Yeah. I guess so."

Beth and the rest of The Fabulous Five cheered. When the phone started ringing, Brittany dashed toward it. "It's probably for me," she called out.

But she was back a moment later. "Hey, Beth, it's for you." She sounded disappointed.

Beth hurried to the phone. "Hello?"

"Beth?" the voice said. "This is Whitney Larkin."

"Oh, hi, Whitney!" Beth said. "How are you?"

"Fine. I just saw your Junque Jewelry on TV, and I

love it," said Whitney. "Do you think you could make a pair of earrings for me? I mean, I'd pay you to make them."

"Really?" Beth could hardly believe her ears. "Well, sure, I'd be glad to. I'll let you know the price after I decide what to use to make them."

"Terrific!" Whitney replied. "Thanks, Beth. I can't wait to see them."

"Guess what!" Beth cried excitedly as she ran back to the living room. The rest of her family had scattered to various parts of the house, so The Fabulous Five were alone. "Whitney Larkin just called and asked me to make her a pair of earrings. And she's going to pay me!"

"You've been commissioned," Christie said.

"What?" Beth asked.

"Great artists are commissioned to do work for people," Christie explained. "And now you're being commissioned to make Junque Jewelry."

Katie let out a low whistle. "That's fantastic."

The telephone rang again, and in a moment Mrs. Barry called out, "Beth! It's for you!"

Beth ran to the phone.

"Beth? You don't know me, but I'm a ninth-grader at Wakeman. My name is Jennifer Perkins, and I just saw you on TV and wondered if you'd consider selling some of your earrings."

"Oh!" Beth said, startled. *Another commission!* "Sure. I'd be glad to sell you some."

"Great," said Jennifer. "Could you bring some to school so I can choose?"

"You bet," Beth said. Her head was spinning. She was actually going to earn money selling her earrings! Breathlessly, she told her friends the news. She was going to sell earrings to someone she didn't even know.

"It's incredible!" Beth added. "I can't believe these people want to buy Junque Jewelry."

"Why not?" asked Katie. "They know a good thing when they see it. Besides, it's a bargain."

"I think it's great," said Jana. "You'll be able to pay back your parents even faster."

"You're right," Beth said. "Talk about miracles."

The telephone rang again, and this time it was Kaci Davis, who wanted a gold necklace and earrings made out of tangled fishing line.

"Beth, we'll see you later," Jana said. "We don't want to get in the way of a budding career."

"Just think," Christie commented. "Wakeman's own entrepreneur!"

*　　*　　*

By lunchtime Beth had taken orders for over ten pairs of earrings and several necklaces. Deciding she'd better get started on the work, she hurried down to the basement. She met her mother coming up the stairs carrying a laundry basket piled high with clothes fresh from the dryer.

"You'll never guess what, Mom! All those phone calls? They were from people who saw the show and wanted to order Junque Jewelry from me!"

Her mother's mouth fell open. "Wonderful!"

"I'm going to be able to pay you back in a *much* shorter time than I had thought," Beth said, beaming.

Her mother laughed. "Well, Junque Jewelry to the rescue!"

"You said it," Beth said.

Mrs. Barry started up the stairs.

"Mom?" Beth called, just as her mother reached the top.

Mrs. Barry turned. "Hmmmm?"

"Thanks," said Beth.

"For what?"

Beth smiled sheepishly. "For bailing me out with my debts. I didn't say thank you before because I was too caught up in how miserable I was going to be."

Mrs. Barry smiled warmly at her daughter. "You're welcome, honey."

Just then the phone rang.

"Don't you think you'd better get it?" her mother asked, grinning. "It's probably for you."

"Right!" shouted Beth. She maneuvered past her mother on the stairs and hurried on up to answer the phone, calling over her shoulder, "Make way for Beth Barry, ENTREPRENEUR!"

Mr. Levine lifted his paper cup filled with root beer. "Congratulations, folks, on our first month of productions. I think our first four shows were excellent, and you all deserve this little celebration."

The students in the Media Club cheered. They had met at Pizza Perfect after the final shoot of the month. Friends were welcome, so Beth had invited The Fabulous Five to join the group.

"I can't believe a whole month has gone by!" said Beth. "It went so fast!"

Shawnie nodded. "It seems as if we shot the first show just last week."

"But on Monday," Mr. Levine went on, "it will be time to get to work again on our next month of *The Wakeman Bulletin Board*. All of you will have the opportunity to see Funny and Shane on TV—"

"I'm going to be a star," Shane said with just a trace of a smile.

"I can't *wait*," Melanie whispered to Beth.

Beth squeezed Melanie's arm affectionately.

"And," Mr. Levine continued, "I think they will do a super job. Beth will be directing, Tim will operate the camera, Jon will have the ecology segment, and Paul and Shawnie will be reporters."

"Sounds like another great lineup," Jana said to Beth.

Mr. Levine heard her remark. "I agree," he said, and looked around the room. "On that note, I'd like to adjourn. It's been a great first month, gang. Let's keep it up!"

The whole group burst into applause. Then the sounds of chairs scraping the floor and talk and laughter filled the small room while the kids got up to go home.

Beth, Jana, Christie, Katie, and Melanie strolled out of Pizza Perfect's front door together and into the evening air. The sun was sitting on the horizon like a huge yellow balloon.

Beth sighed. "That was quite a month. Fun, exciting, terrifying, and *educational*!"

Jana laughed. "Well, it had a happy ending. That's what counts."

"I guess you're right," said Beth.

"We're so proud of you, Beth," Christie said.

Beth turned to Christie. "Thanks," she replied, her cheeks tinting pink with pleasure.

"That's right," added Katie. "You were polished, and poised, and a real pro."

Beth stopped walking and looked around at her friends. "Thanks, guys," she said. "But I'm the proud one. You're always there for me. Whether it's to support me when I perform, or to lend me money, or to just be there when I need a friend. I'm so proud to be one of The Fabulous Five!"

The girls grinned back at her. Then they locked arms and headed toward home.

CHAPTER

14

*K*atie Shannon ran a brush through her red hair and glanced at her watch.

"Eeek," she said half aloud. "I didn't realize that it was so late. Tony should have been here already."

She raced down the stairs and grabbed a jacket from the hall closet.

"How do I look?" Katie asked her mother who was watching her from the kitchen.

Willie smiled. "Great, honey. What movie are you and Tony going to see tonight?"

"It's a thriller called *Follow Me Quietly*, and the theater absolutely will not let anyone in after it starts. Not only that, but they say the ending is so surprising that you're not supposed to tell anyone what happens after you see it."

"Sounds good," said her mother, raising an eyebrow.

Katie nodded and looked out the window. She couldn't wait to see the movie. She had had to convince Tony to give up watching a baseball game to go, but she knew he'd be glad that he did. Besides, that was all he had been doing lately. She was starting to feel as if he liked baseball more than he liked her.

Where is he anyway? she wondered. They had only twenty minutes left to get to the theater before the movie started. They would barely make it in time.

"Is Tony late?" asked Willie, seeing her look out the window again for Tony.

"Um-hm." Katie sighed. It wasn't like Tony to be late. And tonight, of all nights, when they were supposed to see *Follow Me Quietly.*

Ten minutes later Katie picked up the receiver and punched in the first three digits of Tony's number, then hung up. If something really is wrong, she thought, he would have called me.

She went back to the window, trying not to look at her watch. Slowly she began to make out a figure running up the street. It was Tony.

Katie called "Good-bye" to her mother and hurried

out the door. She met Tony just as he reached her front sidewalk.

"Where have you been?" she demanded.

Tony struggled to catch his breath. "Gosh, Katie . . . I'm sorry . . . but there was this baseball game on TV . . . and I couldn't leave . . ."

Katie looked at him in astonishment. "Do you mean to say that you're late because of some stupid baseball game? Do you realize that we'll probably miss the movie?"

"Yeah, but, Katie," he went on breathlessly, "you wouldn't believe the game José Canseco was having! Every time the Yankees got a run, Canseco drove in a run. The score was two to two, three to three, then five to five. Finally, he got a grand slammer in the eighth and put the game away. It was out of sight! I just had to watch." A sheepish expression crossed his face. "It won't happen again. I promise! This was absolutely the last time."

Katie's anger faded. Tony really looked sorry.

But will Tony live up to his promise? What will happen if Katie gets fed up with competing with television for Tony's attention? Find out in The Fabulous Five #24: *The Great TV Turnoff.*

ABOUT THE AUTHOR

Betsy Haynes, the daughter of a former newswoman, began scribbling poetry and short stories as soon as she learned to write. A serious writing career, however, had to wait until after her marriage and the arrival of her two children. But that early practice must have paid off, for within three months Mrs. Haynes had sold her first story. In addition to a number of magazine short stories and the Taffy Sinclair series, Mrs. Haynes is also the author of *The Great Mom Swap* and its sequel, *The Great Boyfriend Trap*. She lives in Marco Island, Florida, with her husband, who is also an author.

Taffy Sinclair is perfectly gorgeous and totally stuck-up. Ask her rival Jana Morgan or anyone else in the sixth grade of Mark Twain Elementary. Once you meet Taffy, life will **never** be the same.

Don't Miss Any of the Terrific Taffy Sinclair Titles from Betsy Haynes!

- ☐ 15819 **TAFFY GOES TO HOLLYWOOD** $2.95
- ☐ 15712 **THE AGAINST TAFFY SINCLAIR CLUB** $2.75
- ☐ 15693 **BLACKMAILED BY TAFFY SINCLAIR** $2.75
- ☐ 15604 **TAFFY SINCLAIR AND THE MELANIE MAKEOVER** $2.75
- ☐ 15644 **TAFFY SINCLAIR AND THE ROMANCE MACHINE DISASTER** $2.75
- ☐ 15714 **TAFFY SINCLAIR AND THE SECRET ADMIRER EPIDEMIC** $2.75
- ☐ 15713 **TAFFY SINCLAIR, BABY ASHLEY AND ME** $2.75
- ☐ 15647 **TAFFY SINCLAIR, QUEEN OF THE SOAPS** $2.75
- ☐ 15645 **TAFFY SINCLAIR STRIKES AGAIN** $2.75
- ☐ 15607 **THE TRUTH ABOUT TAFFY SINCLAIR** $2.75

Follow the adventures of Jana and the rest of **THE FABULOUS FIVE** in a new series by Betsy Haynes.

— — — — — — — — — — — — — — — — —

Bantam Books, Dept. SK26, 414 East Golf Road, Des Plaines, IL 60016

Please send me the items I have checked above. I am enclosing $_____ (please add $2.00 to cover postage and handling). Send check or money order, no cash or C.O.D.s please.

Mr/Ms _____

Address _____

City/State _____ Zip _____

SK26-9/90

Please allow four to six weeks for delivery.
Prices and availability subject to change without notice.